For Papa, who loves his veggies!
—B.J.H.

For my lovely boyfriend, Paul
—S.H.

THIS IS A BORZOI BOOK PUBLISHED BY ALFRED A. KNOPF

Text copyright © 2009 by Barbara Jean Hicks
Illustrations copyright © 2009 by Sue Hendra

All rights reserved. Published in the United States by Alfred A. Knopf,
an imprint of Random House Children's Books, a division of Random House, Inc., New York.

Knopf, Borzoi Books, and the colophon are registered trademarks of Random House, Inc.

Visit us on the Web! www.randomhouse.com/kids

Educators and librarians, for a variety of teaching tools, visit us at www.randomhouse.com/teachers

Library of Congress Cataloging-in-Publication Data
Hicks, Barbara Jean.
Monsters don't eat broccoli / by Barbara Jean Hicks ; illustrated by Sue Hendra. — 1st ed.
p.   cm.
Summary: Illustrations and rhyming text reveal how imagination can spice up even the healthiest meal.
ISBN 978-0-375-85686-0 (trade) — ISBN 978-0-375-95686-7 (lib. bdg.)
[1. Stories in rhyme. 2. Monsters—Fiction. 3. Food habits—Fiction.] I. Hendra, Sue, ill. II. Title.
PZ8.3.H5328Mon 2009   [E]—dc22   2008024536

The illustrations in this book were created using gouache.

MANUFACTURED IN CHINA
August 2009
10 9 8 7 6 5 4 3 2 1
First Edition

MONSTERS DON'T eat BROCCOLI

By **Barbara Jean Hicks**

Illustrated by **Sue Hendra**

Alfred A. Knopf New York

The waitress in this restaurant
just doesn't have a clue.

Monsters don't eat broccoli!
How could she think we do?

We'd rather snack on tractors

Enjoy
SteamRollers

or a rocket ship or two,

Enjoy
mRollers

or a wheely, steely stew.

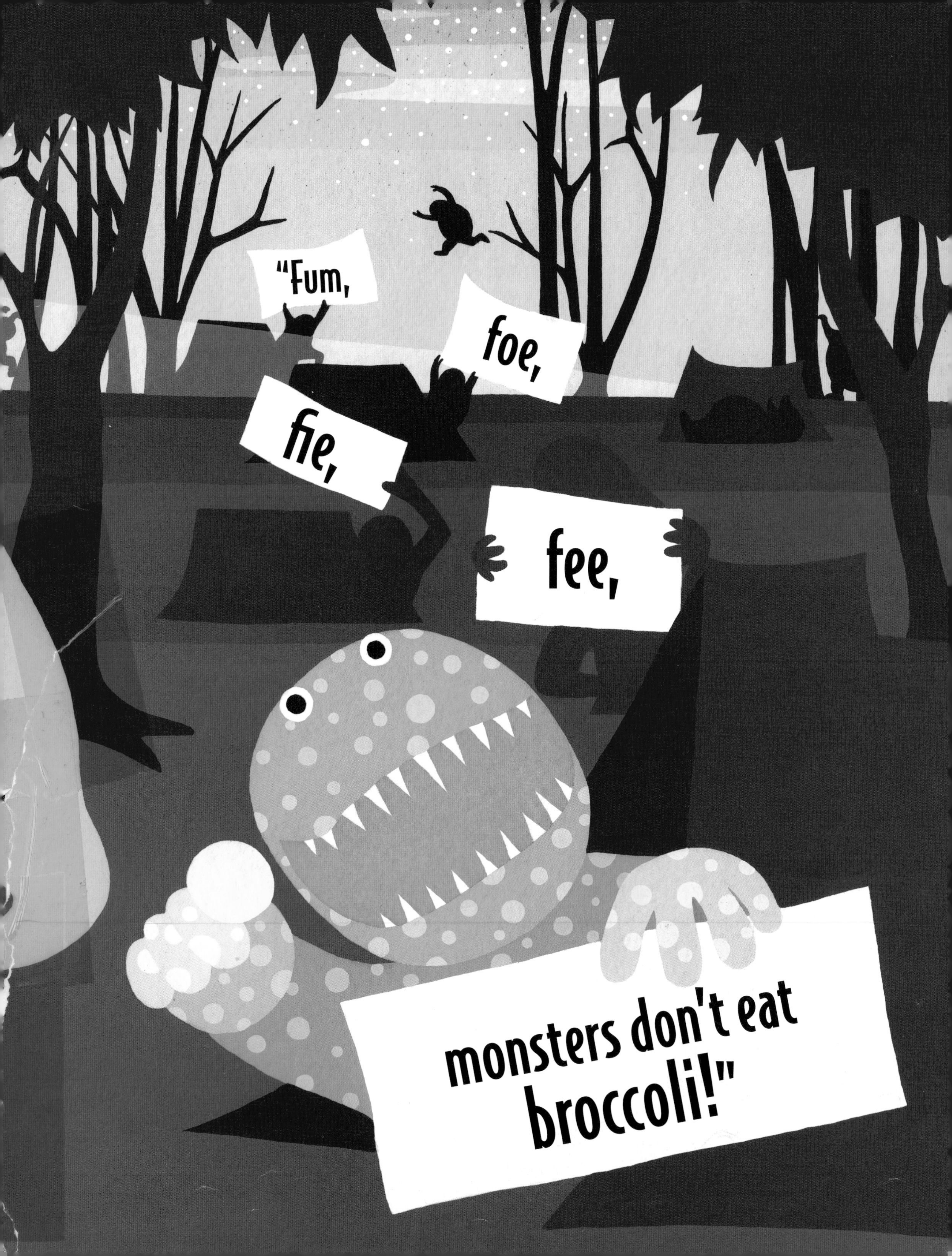
"Fum,
foe,
fie,
fee,
monsters don't eat
broccoli!"

Monsters don't eat broccoli
or artichokes or greens.

We can't abide alfalfa sprouts
or slimy lima beans.

But redwoods are delectable.

And boulders—what a treat!

And a fountain's so refreshing
in this dreadful summer heat.

"Fum, foe, fie, fee,
monsters don't eat broccoli!"

We're crazy for construction,

and we crave our fish 'n' ships—

but monsters don't eat broccoli.
It will not pass our lips.

You cannot force us monsters
to eat vegetables we hate.

Let humans have the garden—
we will eat the garden gate!

Monsters love a picnic
on a blanket in the park,

with a clump of giant maples
and their yummy, gummy bark. . . .

"Fum, foe, fie, fee—
You're chowing
down

Say what? *This* isn't broccoli.
It's crunchy, munchy TREES!

And WOW, are they delicious!

Another helping,

please.

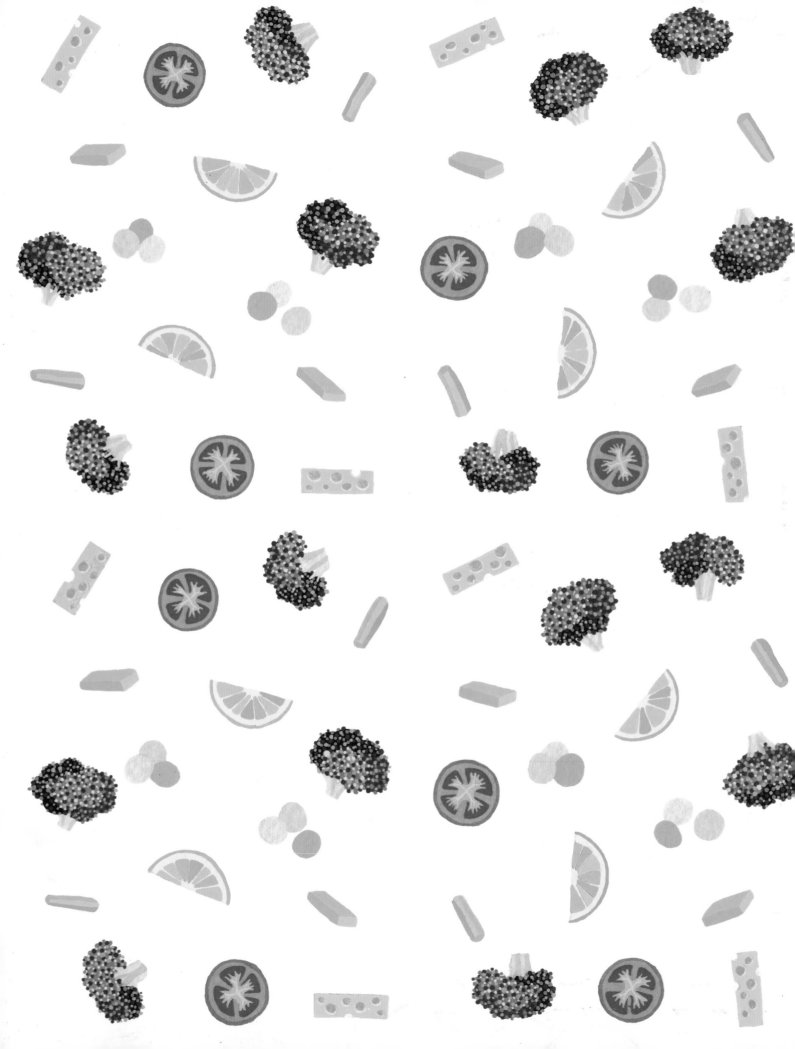